Count Down to Clean Up!

Mae

KJ

"The Twins"

Lila

Henry

Rose

Count Down to Clean Up!

Written and Illustrated by
Nancy Elizabeth Wallace

Houghton Mifflin Company
Boston 2001

Rhea

Roy

William

Carol Ann

Jack

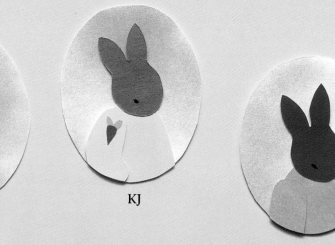

To Joe and Wendy and Helen and David and Lindsay;
Hazel and Paul and Betsy and Chuck and Jane, ten dear friends.
Love, N. E. W.

www.houghtonmifflinbooks.com

The text of this book is set in Goudy.
The illustrations were created using scissors, a glue stick, tape, tweezers, and origami and found paper.

Library of Congress Cataloging-in-Publication Data

Wallace, Nancy Elizabeth.
Count down to clean up! / written and illustrated by Nancy Elizabeth Wallace.
p. cm.
Summary: Little rabbits from one to ten get ready and then help clean up.
ISBN 0-618-10130-6
[1. Rabbits—Fiction. 2. Cleanliness—Fiction. 3. Counting.] I. Title.
PZ7.W15875 Co   2001
[E]—dc21   00-053963

Printed in Singapore
TWP 10 9 8 7 6 5 4 3 2 1

Work Day

Volunteers
needed
to
Clean Up!

Count down to clean up . . .

Ten

BUNNY BUILDING

Nine

Eight

Seven

THE
GOOD SPORT
SHOP

Five

THE BACKYARD
Lawn & Garden Center

Four

Two

One

Betty's Bakery

None

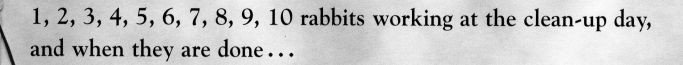

1, 2, 3, 4, 5, 6, 7, 8, 9, 10 rabbits working at the clean-up day, and when they are done...

...it's time to PLAY!

Did you find these?

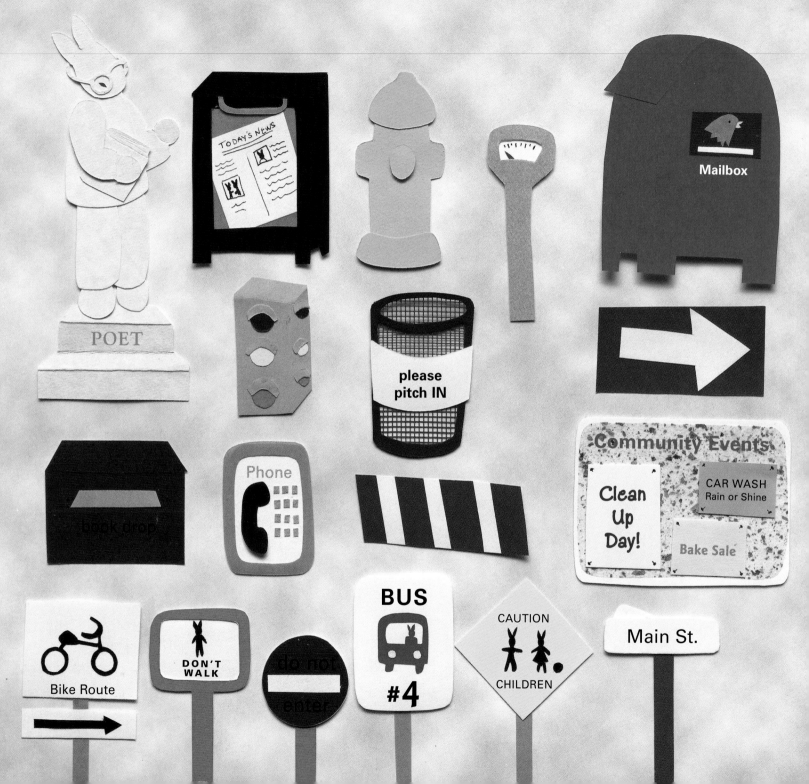